NUDE
COMMUTE

Matador
9 Priory Business Park,
Wistow Road, Kibworth Beauchamp,
Leicestershire. LE8 0RX
Tel: 0116 279 2299
Email: books@troubador.co.uk
Web: www.troubador.co.uk/matador
Twitter: @matadorbooks

ISBN 978 1785893 216

British Library Cataloguing in Publication Data.
A catalogue record for this book is available from the British Library.

Printed and bound by CPI Group (UK) Ltd, Croydon, CR0 4YY
Typeset in 12 pt Gill Sans (T1) by Troubador Publishing Ltd, Leicester, UK

Matador is an imprint of Troubador Publishing Ltd

FSC
www.fsc.org

MIX
Paper from
responsible sources
FSC® C013604

For all commuters everywhere, nude or otherwise…

there is a light at the end of the tunnel.

This quirky tale's of Martin, who lives on the Southern line,

he could have come from anywhere but we wanted it to rhyme.

His surname Matters-Knott, his middle name is Josh,

his mother liked to use it to make them sound quite posh.

He always wears pyjamas when he goes off to his bed,

fleecy ones from M&S with stripes of blue and red.

His mother buys them for him every single year

so Martin has the widest choice a man could wish to wear.

They give him a sense of being tucked in, being read to every night,

which was how he learned *The Tempest* and recites it without sight;

"We are such stuff as dreams are made on," he chants in bardic rhyme

and Dickens too he knows by heart; well not quite every line.

At 6 am and wide awake preparing for the fray,

Martin sits and contemplates another working day.

His chequered slippers lie alert upon the starting grid

whilst he recalls the last night's dreams and the things he did.

Was he with the post room girl on a golden beach

frolicking in the frothy surf with her just out of reach?

Oh! The buxom post room girl, pneumatic and so fair

giving out those envelopes while delivering despair.

And was it Frank playing in the sand with a bouncing ball,

which Martin leapt to catch before embarrassed fall?

Maybe his dream is darker, more meaningful and deep;

Martin tries to analyse the vagaries of sleep.

"Time and tide," thinks Martin as he takes his morning shower,

he puts the plastic hat on to ensure his hair stays drier;

it probably looks ridiculous but no one ever saw

another gift from mummy for her dear boy's bottom drawer.

Martin's in a lather and starts humming through his beard

a tune he barely recognised has suddenly appeared.

"She'll be coming round the mountain," the song mingles with the flow

but why those notes have come to mind he really doesn't know.

Martin sings out loudly, "Aye aye yippee yippee aye!"

until his Pavarotti stance puts soap into his eye.

"There's very little pleasure without resulting pain,"

thinks Martin rather glumly as the suds go down the drain.

It's a form of reassurance as John Humphry's guttural score,

finds its morning audience loyal to Radio Four.

He's an early morning person, not always a jovial host

good at grilling MP's for spreading on his toast.

Martin's trawled the airwaves, finds others somewhat bland

with a condescending DJ playing a contrapuntal band.

He's happy with his cornflakes, his coffee and *Today*,

even though he doesn't gel with everything they say.

The BBC is biased, left wing and run by those

mummy won't approve of and mother always knows.

He contemplates his kitchen with culinary delight

and what he'll cook for supper when he returns tonight.

Always judge a man by the shoes upon his feet,

shiny leather uppers make a man complete.

Doing up his laces and smoothing chequered socks,

Martin's nearly ready and poised on starting blocks.

His flourish to the sportsman, the champ of Formula One,

the socks a winning pattern, a nod to Hamilton.

His racing driver hero is the fastest man he knows,

he's seen him on the telly, seen how fast he goes.

If only he could do it, be quicker than the rest

but first things first thinks Martin, he'd need a driving test.

Martin doesn't drive a car, he gets around on foot

and uses trains and buses to enable his commute.

Stepping out on to the street, he sees the light blue sky,

the fluffy clouds, the rubbish bags and cyclists going by.

The rubbish and the cyclists cause Martin discontent,

both are out of order and on the pavement.

The stuff we seem to throw away is into overload

and why oh why do cyclists never use the road?

He's been to see the council who always seem to fail;

loose paving stones, dirt left by dogs and bundles of junk mail.

Next time he'd put his cross elsewhere, wouldn't vote for them

but it doesn't seem to matter; they're all about the same.

His mother has her standards, never deals with second best

but Martin takes his place in life along with all the rest.

And all the rest or some of them are on their way to work

to earn a worthy shilling or mooch about and shirk.

Everyone looks similar as humans on the move,

some have more accessories with something still to prove.

Shoulder bags and bolder bags, dark glasses without sun,

mobile phones and brollies; Martin carries one.

A fellow on some wheels scoots by like a circus clown

on most erratic transport that could mow pedestrians down.

"Oh those stupid scooters," thinks Martin in a bate,

"if God had wanted us with wheels he'd put them on our feet!

He's showing off that's what it is," mutters Martin in the crowd.

"Why can't he be like us," he thinks. "It shouldn't be allowed."

Every day three million souls do what Martin does

and move into the Underground without a lot of fuss.

It's said to commute is to travel from home to work each day

or reduce judicial sentence from death to lengthy stay.

The lesser of two evils, which is the darkest route,

detained at Her Majesty's pleasure or the Central line commute?

Commuters are not creatures who tunnel where they might,

choosing their direction, straight on or left or right.

Martin and his travellers take the line as laid

if they have their passes and provided they have paid.

Fare dodging's not an option especially if you're caught

so Martin pays and plays the game just as he was taught.

"Please be waiting for one moment," says the burly guard,

keeper of the wire mesh gate, the man looks rather bored.

He's busy with his mobile, more important than the crowd

who wait behind the metal bars yet no one says a word.

Officialdom in a vest that glows holds back the march of men

on their way to make their deals or fill out forms *pro tem*.

They'd rail against the rails penned up like waiting sheep,

but queue in silent order, apart from phones that bleep.

It is the same most mornings and soon the bars subside

and glowing vest waves on the crowd, encourages the tide

that flows below the pavements, beneath the high rise homes

and down into the darkness where man has buried bones.

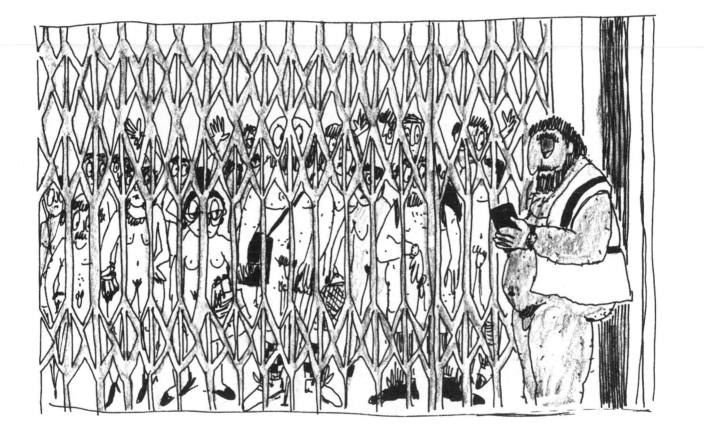

Under starter's orders like horses in the field,

commuters pushing forward, their permits are revealed.

Tickets scanned, passes read, machines will have their fun

by opening up then snapping shut and checking one by one.

There's always one in panic, whose Oyster card has gone;

she thought she had it with her but has left the thing at home.

She's searching for it everywhere, that little piece of card,

rifling in her giant bag, the hunt looks quite absurd.

Martin thinks he'll help her out; she seems in some distress

but his attention misconstrued could cause him some duress.

It's often better not to help and Martin hurries on;

no time for senseless stopping now; no good Samaritan.

The lift descends, as they do, transporting them below

like miners to the working face with pickaxes for coal

and everyone has a fixed stare as sliding underground

no one dares to say a word or make the slightest sound.

The reader in the corner is intent on someone's yarns,

engrossed in a biography or maybe Julian Barnes.

Martin's keen to learn what riveting literary plot

keeps a reader so engaged and glued to what he's got.

Surreptitiously he sneaks a peek and in the flickering lights

sees the paperback is called, *A Hundred Erotic Nights*.

Never can you ever judge a book just by its cover

nor the reader it would seem; he looked like any other.

"Things have rather escalated," says a man on Martin's left.

"It's all going down if you see what I mean," the fellow then confessed.

Martin doesn't say a word as personal communication

to any stranger on the move might meet with condemnation.

It's bad enough travelling with such boorish folk

but when they try and talk to you it's really not a joke.

Who on earth they think they are and what gives them the right

to invade a person's privacy when it's already rather tight.

Martin tries to ignore the man by looking at those ads,

the ones for shows and chocolate bars and palmtop gaming pads.

He doesn't really need a loan but there's no doubting if he does,

the nice man from Sillyloans.com would do it without a fuss.

Arriving on the platform is a venture much the same,

one always gets there just in time to see the leaving train.

Martin stands and waits; the waiting takes so long

with so much more time standing still than time spent moving on.

If only there were other ways, thinks Martin as he waits,

for quickly getting to your work without frustrating traits.

Like that thing in *Star Trek* that teleports the crew,

"Beam me up please Scotty. Beam me up please do."

He dreams of telecommuting, of getting there like mail

but would the post room's handling cause his wooer's heart to fail?

With happy thoughts of being handled by his post room muse,

Martin awaits another train for everyone to use.

And with a gust of tunnel wind in slides the sparking beast

to much anticipation for some standing room at least.

Noisy breaks on rails, the tube pulls to a halt

and then the doors slide open with a sudden jolt.

Martin is never near one, it never works for him,

he's half way between two open doors, neither welcoming.

He does that sideways shuffle, that silly platform dance

along with all the others, each tries to grab their chance.

But before the scrum can muster, before the push and fight,

there are passengers who've had enough pleading to alight.

So like a brief encounter as a line at a Highland fling,

two ranks will face each other, poised before the din.

Then comes the hurly burly and the need to get inside

as if their lives depended on this last eternal ride.

Martin stays on one side of the heaving and the slap,

hears those grunts and groans and pleas of, "Mind the gap!"

They might have been at Twickenham although the sign says not.

He doesn't play a contact sport; it doesn't float his boat.

Martin thinks that some of them, the pushers in the main,

enjoy the participation and rather like the game.

So too some of those being shoved, pushed at from behind,

they seem to take it in their stride, no one seems to mind.

Like the stuffing of a turkey or the filling of a cake,

people find their portions and take up the space they make.

There's room for nearly everyone like clothes hung out to dry

swinging from the overheads and standing eye to eye.

Martin has got used to it and the pungent nasal wave

of different body odours and ghastly aftershave.

He travels a few stations with an armpit in his face,

an elbow and a rucksack encroaching on his space.

The hair of some that have it is like a janitor's mop,

lank and greasy, all unkempt, with dirty bits on top.

They're all in this together going forward cheek by jowl,

going forward for a shilling and that fortnight in Funchal;

stuck like toothpaste in the tube waiting for the squeeze

that one day will release them and push them out with ease.

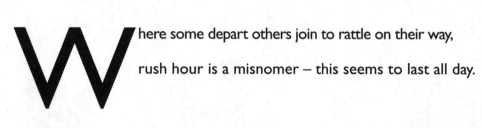

Where some depart others join to rattle on their way,

rush hour is a misnomer – this seems to last all day.

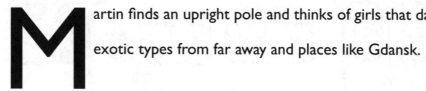

Martin finds an upright pole and thinks of girls that dance, exotic types from far away and places like Gdansk.

t last a seat is vacant and Martin settles down

and studies those around him travelling beneath this town.

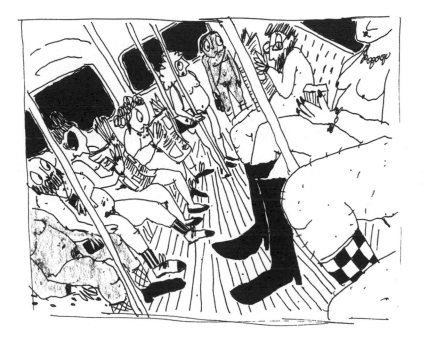

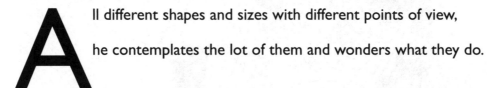

All different shapes and sizes with different points of view,

he contemplates the lot of them and wonders what they do.

nd when the lights start flickering, stutter and then fail,

everyone is shrouded by that all pervasive veil.

Then they come back on again and everyone is back

from all the trepidation of their journey in the black.

At his destination he steps out through the doors

and walks along the platform until he has to pause.

A young man approaches him with an urgent task,

"Is this Cockfosters?" Martin hears him ask.

Martin wants to tell him, "No. It belongs to me,"

but doesn't bother to respond to the fellow's plea.

When overfriendly strangers suddenly appear

maybe picking pockets, it's time to be aware.

So Martin takes the exit and walks with heavy tread,

his working day may not be good, he views it with some dread.

He has a big agenda, a presentation to his board,

he's worried what he has to say might be totally ignored.

46

Music from a busker echoes off the walls,

"Bien joué!" says Martin as a gesture of applause.

Martin admires an instrument handled with acclaim

but despite his mother's begging he never did the same.

He stroked and plucked at all the strings his mother could provide

but made a noise like alley cats committing suicide.

Martin drops a coin or two down onto the floor.

"My grandfuzzer wus in the underground during the last war."

"Marquis?" asks Martin politely, he'd seen *The Longest Day*.

"Metro," says the busker and continues with his play.

Martin sees the irony but doesn't stop to talk,

he has more pressing issues and worries over work.

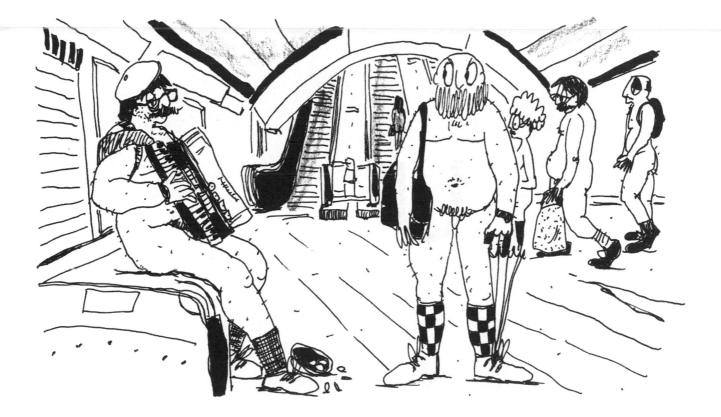

Up the escalator.

p the healthy stair.

e exits through the barrier.

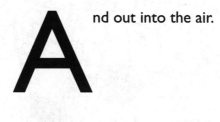

And out into the air.

And joins the throng of people walking as they can

at the intersection with that flashing man.

Everyone has purpose, a task to undergo

but Martin has an anxious look, he really doesn't know

how his day will unfold, if he can pull the strings

or if the firm he works for has plans for other things.

He's been a tireless servant for nigh on twenty years,

will get a decent pension if he's paid up the arrears.

With fear of being redundant or past his sell by date,

Martin strides off to his desk; he'd better not be late.

It's eight thirty seven precisely and he's sitting in his slot

behind the name he has on it, M.J. Matters-Knott.

He's turned on his computer, gives his mail a glance,

it's very unimportant and from a smaller branch.

He's been the menswear buyer for this high street fashion chain

and today they are considering their look for future gain.

They've always been quite mainstream and not considered niche,

their target market is the men who eat both steak and quiche.

But in the current climate where everyone is nude,

Martin isn't confident, his thinkng may be skewed.

Sales have slumped to zero with business in the red.

"Bottom's fallen out o'market," is what the Chairman said.

Frank his fit assistant who works out in the gym

joins Martin in his office to go through everything.

"We've got this presentation, Frank. I'm feeling sort of there

but with a nagging doubt or two we're chasing the right hare?"

Frank who has ambition didn't want to say

what he thought of Martin's plans; he rather liked his pay

and if his boss looked silly as well he might quite soon,

Frank may get promoted and that would be a boon.

"I think your ideas are sound," he said, "you'll wow them with your style."

He flashed his boss a big broad grin, his Caribbean smile.

"Oh by the way, the post room girl has got a thing for you."

Martin's heart leapt to his mouth and skipped a beat or two.

The post room girl is putting all the envelopes to bed

and Martin has an image that comes racing to his head.

He stutters to the post room girl, "You've got a thing for me."

She turns and says, "Perhaps I have. Let's have a look and see."

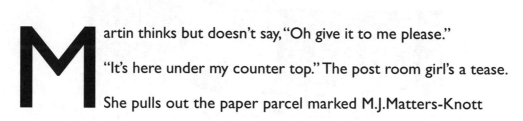

Martin thinks but doesn't say, "Oh give it to me please."

"It's here under my counter top." The post room girl's a tease.

She pulls out the paper parcel marked M.J.Matters-Knott

and hands it to poor Martin who sees that's all he's got.

"Thank you for the package," says Martin all polite;

he really wants to have a date with her next Friday night.

"Would you like to… see what I've got?" he says losing all his nerve.

But the girl just turns and walks away with accentuated verve.

Martin takes his parcel to the locker room and sighs;

the fragrance of the post room girl, her warm and friendly eyes.

Will he ever ask her out and what if she says yes?

There is no doubt in Martin's mind one day she'll acquiesce,

especially when she sees him with what he has in mind,

the contents of his package will make her quite inclined.

So he rips the paper open, it's time to do the deed,

it's time to take the contents out and sow the latest seed.

He feels he's on the grid at the start of this Grand Prix,

it was now or never, do or die, he really had to see

and out from that brown paper his future does unfold

but will his innovation prove to be too bold?

So just before the meeting, the one on the top floor,

Martin slips into the suit he's tried just once before.

It fits him like a good suit should, cut from Savile Row,

although of course he's kept the price reasonably low.

He's nervous as a kitten and straightens out the tie,

the one his mother got for him; he didn't have to buy.

The shirt of finest cotton is folded with those pins

and bits of card and plastic that end up in the bins.

The black shoes are of leather made in Northamptonshire

by cobblers who are craftsmen. They make their shoes with care.

Martin then considers his morning's nude commute

and whether it will catch on, the tube-inspired new suit?

The boardroom presentation doesn't go as he has planned

in fact the raucous laughter gets somewhat out of hand.

The Chairman hurts his rib cage with all of his guffaws

while the FD laughs like one of those whose laughs are mixed with snores.

The head of Human Resources is simply lost for speech

but supportive of her Chairman, she too begins to screech,

and Sandra taking minutes is not sure what to put

and enters in her records, "He wore a phallic suit."

Shouts the marketing director, whose own job's on the line,

"You look an utter knob man, though the cut is rather fine."

Martin says that his design called *Travelling Underground*

might encourage dressing up instead of dressing down.

As the deafening laughter dies, subsides a notch or three

and tears roll down the bosses' cheeks and drip into their tea,

Martin is incredulous, regards them with disdain;

surely they're all wrong he thinks; we will wear clothes again.

The tube-lined tailored suit for him, haute couture for her,

the things we used to dress up in, those clothes of yesteryear;

cavalry twill and corduroy, the blazer and stay-pressed slacks;

a hacking jacket in Harris Tweed and matching natty caps,

the double-breasted overcoat, woollen cardigan

and underpants that give support to every shape of man.

Some will take the tartan and make themselves the kilt,

where underneath nothing's worn. It's as good as the day it was built.

"Martin!" says the Chairman, "I think we're all agreed

that dressing up has gone away. There no longer is the need.

With that in mind dear boy," he says, "review your current thoughts."

So Martin leaves the boardroom feeling very out of sorts.

He heads back to his office with his tail between his legs

and then into the locker room to change out of his threads.

He cannot show the post room girl his triumph has gone flat

and she will only see him for a guy who's rather fat,

who hasn't got the sort of thing that other men possess,

which turns the heads of all the girls; or those that they impress.

The only lady companion who will never do Martin wrong

is his dearest mother, so he calls her on the phone.

Martin leaves the building at the close of play.

What a fruitless enterprise! What a dreadful day!

He bins the tube-lined failure, sets off in pouring rain,

the evening sky's in sympathy with Martin's inner pain.

They march along like soldiers, umbrellas open wide

to keep the rain from wetting them and damping down their pride.

And wouldn't it be better, thought Martin on the hoof,

if everyone out in the rain could wear a waterproof.

The trouble with umbrellas is a sudden windy gust

might turn the world inside out; expose you to the worst.

Of course this happens to Martin and just to make his day,

his one form of protection snaps and blows away.

His journey home is dreary and he takes the Underground

which he finds quite suitable, appropriate and profound.

His life is like a tube train stuck upon its rail,

with one direction only, one line that leads to "Fail."

And all these nude commuters naked just like him

have ups and downs and good and bad and never wear a thing.

We come into this world with nothing on at all,

so why dress up what's underneath and bow to Adam's fall?

And with this thought he trundles on, it's no good to complain with one of those and two of those we're really all the same. Different shapes and sizes with different temperaments, we're all in this together, all *Homo sapiens*.

When he reaches his station, the one on the Southern line,

he has to make a dash for it to try and dodge the rain

and then he sees the lady, the one he knows so well,

his mother's touting lifeboat flags but they are hard to sell.

"Hello mother," says Martin, "you'll find it rather rare

to sell these things to passers-by who insist on being bare."

"Quite so, dear," says his mother. "It really is a shame

there's nowhere for them to stick the pin and everyone's the same.

If only people dressed properly like they used to do

we could sell more lifeboat pins to build more lifeboats too!"

It was like a flash of lightning, a eureka moment struck

and Martin knew there and then how he'd change his luck.

It was a cross between a waistcoat and those jackets worn at sea

with wide lapels and pockets and storage facility.

It was just the blooming ticket for keeping tickets safe,

for pinning little badges on and storing bits of cake

and cheese and pickle sandwiches packed safely for that snack;

it could also hold a waterproof should the weather need a mac

and if you were a busker you'd have a place for notes,

somewhere safe to store the coins and keep those king-sized tokes.

Martin's new invention is fashion with attitude

ideal for those who need it while travelling in the nude.

He'd show those boardroom Jonnies so dismissive of his plan.

His would be the last laugh! He would be the man!

He'd quit his job as buyer and start his own affair

making things called, *Matters-Knott* for everyone to wear.

He realised that he'd gone too far, his ill-conceived tube suit

was superfluous and unnecessary for those who nude commute.

He dreamed of making money and the thoughts it would invoke

and how he and the post room girl could slope off and elope.

She'd have to settle down with him and forsaking every other,

move into his home with him and of course his mother.

He'd never have to travel on the Underground again,

would take on Frank as chauffer to drive his Mercedes Benz.

It would have a private number plate marked MJMK 1

and everyone would nod at him, the tycoon he'd become.

Martin slips into bed wrapped up in M&S

and ponders on his pillow the secret of success.

His life is back on track again or that's how it would seem,

unless it's all a twist of fate, some convoluted dream?

Clothing gives us badges and cloth to hide behind,

to mask our insecurities and give us peace of mind.

For if we all went naked about our daily lives

how different the world might be with fewer concealing lies.

So when next you sit on the tube and look around and stare,

imagine what we'd all look like with nothing on, quite bare.

Does it matter what you dress like, clothes or birthday suit

as underneath what ever it is, we all just nude commute?

Charlie Berridge wrote the words.

Hannah Carding drew the pictures.